Christmas Mice!

Christmas Mice!

by Bethany Roberts

Illustrated by Doug Cushman

Green Light Readers
HOUGHTON MIFFLIN HARCOURT
Boston   New York

www.hmhco.com

The Library of Congress has cataloged the hardcover edition as follows:
Roberts, Bethany.
Christmas Mice!/by Bethany Roberts; illustrated by Doug Cushman.
p. cm.
Summary: A group of mice have fun as they go about their preparations for Christmas.
[1. Mice—Fiction. 2. Christmas—Fiction. 3. Stories in rhyme.]
I. Cushman, Doug, ill. II. Title.
PZ8.3.R5295 Ch 2000
[E]—21 98-51133

ISBN: 978-0-395-91204-1 hardcover
ISBN: 978-0-618-48601-4 paperback
ISBN: 978-0-544-34104-3 GLR paperback
ISBN: 978-0-544-34102-9 GLR paper over board

Manufactured in China
SCP 10 9 8 7 6 5 4 3 2 1

4500476223

To Melissa—Merry Christmas
—B.R.

To Valerie and Monica and the gang at Hicklebees
—D.C.

Christmas mice
deck the house.

Wreath the door.
Pound, pound, pound!

Christmas mice
wrap lots of presents.

Shiny ribbons,
round and round!

Christmas mice
trim the tree.

Put a star
on the top, top, top!

Christmas mice
bake yummy goodies.

Flour everywhere.
Mop, mop, mop!

Christmas secrets.
Stop! Don't peek!

Now out in the snow
to sing, sing, sing!

Merry, merry!
Joy, joy, joy!

Jingle bells!
Ring, ring, ring!

Across the sky—
a spot, a streak.

"Peace to all!"
Did you hear that?

Look—a paw print
in the snow.

Someone's been here!
Yikes! The cat!

What's this? A gift!
"From Cat to Mice."

A Christmas cheese!
Oh, yum, yum, yum!

The cat has caught
our Christmas cheer!

Now let's thank
our new-found chum.

Wrap one last gift—
"From Mice to Cat."

Tie it with
a big red bow.

Leave it here,
right by her door.

"Merry Christmas—"

"Ho, ho, ho!"